Disappearing Dreams!

Chet dropped his dream recipe in the empty shopping cart. Just then a voice came over the loudspeaker. "Attention shoppers!" it said. "Pick up free cookie samples in aisle five."

"Cookies?" Chet cried. He began to run. "I'm there!"

Frank and Joe ran after Chet. But as they ran up aisle five, Frank stopped.

"Wait, you guys," he said. "We left the shopping cart alone."

"And my recipe!" Chet said.

The boys raced back to the shopping cart. It was empty.

"Uh-oh," Joe said with a gulp.

"My dream pizza recipe," Chet said. His voice cracked. "It's gone!"

Frank and Joe Hardy: The Clues Brothers

Avaiable from MINSTREL BOOKS

THE PUMPED-UP PIZZA PROBLEM

Franklin W. Dixon

Illustrated by
Marcy Ramsey

A
MINSTREL®
BOOK

Published by POCKET BOOKS
New York   London   Toronto   Sydney   Tokyo   Singapore

This book is a work of fiction. Names, characters, places and incidents are products of the author's imagination or are used fictitiously. Any resemblance to actual events or locales or persons living or dead is entirely coincidental.

A MINSTREL PAPERBACK *Original*

A Minstrel Book published by
POCKET BOOKS, a division of Simon & Schuster Inc.
1230 Avenue of the Americas, New York, NY 10020

Copyright © 1998 by Simon & Schuster Inc.

ISBN: 0-671-02142-7

First Minstrel Books printing November 1998

10 9 8 7 6 5 4 3 2 1

FRANK AND JOE HARDY: THE CLUES BROTHERS is a trademark of Simon & Schuster Inc.

THE HARDY BOYS, A MINSTREL BOOK and colophon are registered trademarks of Simon & Schuster Inc.

Cover art by Thompson Studio

Printed in the U.S.A.

1

Pizza Pies . . . Pizza Prize

I wonder what the Power Patrol will morph into today," nine-year-old Frank Hardy said.

"Maybe skeletons," his eight-year-old brother, Joe, said. "*Invisible* skeletons!"

Their friend Kevin Saris wrinkled his nose. "How would anyone know they're skeletons if they're invisible?" he asked.

The boys' other friend Chet Morton shrugged. "Their bones would rattle."

It was Friday afternoon. The boys were seated on the couch in the Hardys' den, watching their favorite TV show, *The Pumped-Up Power Patrol.*

Joe turned to Frank. "Don't you wish we could turn into things when we solve mysteries?" he asked.

Frank nodded. He and Joe loved solving mysteries more than anything. Those who knew Frank and Joe liked to call them the Clues Brothers.

Their dad, Fenton Hardy, was a detective in Bayport. He often helped them with their cases.

"Check it out," Kevin said. "Pumped-Up Pete is turning into a ball of flames."

"Hot stuff!" Chet shouted.

The boys cheered as the human fireball rolled toward the enemy. Suddenly the words "We'll Be Right Back" flashed on the screen.

"Another commercial?" Joe groaned.

"I like commercials," Chet said. He stood up from the couch. "They give me time to grab a snack."

"Wait!" Joe shouted. He pulled Chet

back on the couch. "The Power Patrol is in this commercial."

Frank stared at the TV. "And they're holding up pizzas," he said.

"Now, that's what I call a TV dinner," Chet said. He smacked his lips.

"Hey, kids," Pumped-Up Pete said. "Check out our new frozen pizzas."

"*Frozen* pizzas?" Kevin asked.

Kevin knew everything about pizzas. His parents owned Pizza Paradise. Sometimes he helped them bake the pies.

"Pumped-Up Power Pizzas are coming to your grocery store!" Pumped-Up Phil said.

"There'll be all kinds," Pumped-Up Pablo said. "Like Pumped-Up Pepperoni, Mighty Mushroom, and Broccoli Blast!"

"If you think that's cool," Pumped-Up Pierre said, "we're having a contest for the best pizza you kids can cook up."

"If your pizza wins," Pumped-Up Phil went on, "you'll get to appear on—"

3

"The Pumped-Up Power Patrol show!" they shouted together.

"All right!" Joe shouted.

"We'll be at the Bayport Mall this Sunday to choose the best pizza," Pumped-Up Pablo said. "So pick up the rules at the Ripe Apple Supermarket and get cookin'."

Frank, Joe, and Chet jumped up from the couch. They gave one another high fives.

"Let's go for it," Frank said.

Chet nodded. "We love pizza. And with Kevin on our team, how can we lose?"

Kevin slumped back on the couch. "Who said I was entering the contest?" he asked.

"You don't want to enter?" Joe asked.

"Why not?" Frank asked.

Kevin jumped up from the couch. "Because those Pumped-Up Power Pizzas are going to put Pizza Paradise out of business!" he said.

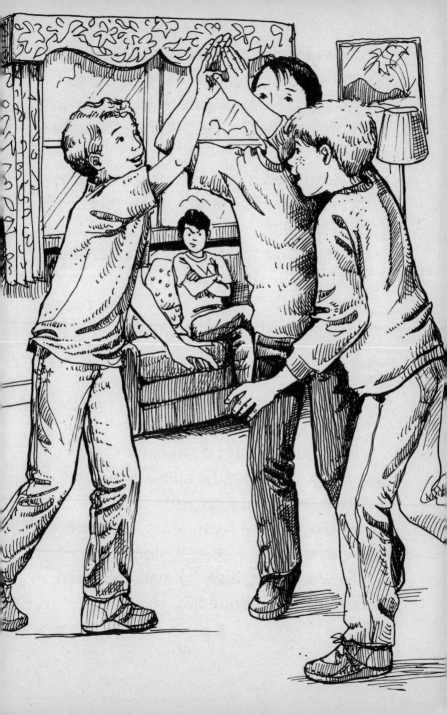

Joe wiped his forehead. All the letter *p*'s in the sentence had made Kevin spit.

"No way," Frank said. "Everyone in Bayport knows that Pizza Paradise rules."

Chet nodded. "Just because those guys turn into fireballs doesn't mean they can cook," he said.

Kevin shook his head. "If I enter that contest, I'd be a big traitor."

"But, Kevin," Frank said. "The prize is a chance to be on the show."

"Yeah," Chet said. "They might even give us free pizzas—"

Joe gave Chet a quick nudge.

"I mean, free autographs," Chet said.

"If you don't want us to enter the contest, we won't," Frank told Kevin.

Kevin walked toward the door of the den. "Do whatever you want," he said.

"Where are you going?" Joe asked.

"To Pizza Paradise," Kevin muttered. "While it's still around."

Frank, Joe, and Chet looked at one another.

"Wait, Kevin," Frank called. "We'll walk out with you."

All four boys walked quietly out of the house.

"Does that mean he's not on our team?" Chet asked when Kevin was down the block.

Frank shrugged. "He didn't tell us not to enter," he said.

"But how are we going to make a pizza without Kevin?" Joe asked.

"That's probably the easy part," Frank said. "First we have to come up with a great idea."

The three boys sat down on the Hardys' doorstep.

"How about a pizza with hot dogs, mustard, and relish?" Joe asked. "We can call it the Meanie-Weenie Pie."

"I got it!" Chet shouted. "A pizza—with five different kinds of ice cream."

"Gross me out," Frank groaned.

Joe nudged Frank. "Speaking of gross, look who's coming."

Frank looked up. Zack Jackson was riding his bike up the Hardys' front walk.

"Hardy-Har-Har!" Zack sneered.

Zack was the biggest bully at Bayport Elementary School. He and his bad-news friends called themselves the Zack Pack.

"What are you working on now, Clues Brothers?" Zack asked. He looked at Chet. "The case of Morton's missing brain?"

Chet tapped his head with his finger. "Oh, yeah? It takes a brain to come up with a prizewinning pizza," he said.

Zack's eyes opened wide. "You're entering the Pumped-Up Power Pizza contest?" he asked. "No way!"

Joe nodded. "We've already come up with a zillion awesome ideas."

Zack waved his hand. It was covered with stick-on tattoos. "Ah, you don't have a chance," he said.

"Oh, yeah?" Frank asked. "How come?"

"Because me and my friends are entering the contest, too," Zack said.

"The Zack Pack?" Frank laughed.

"The only thing you guys can cook up is trouble," Joe said.

Zack spun his bike around. "Well, don't count on winning," he called over his shoulder. *"Losers* never do!"

The boys watched Zack zoom away.

"Now we really have to come up with a great pizza idea," Joe groaned.

"But we didn't even get past the crust!" Chet cried.

The boys thought some more. But all they came up with were pizzas topped with baloney and fish sticks.

"Fish sticks on a pizza?" Joe said.

Chet looked at his watch. "Oh, well. I'd better go home for dinner," he said.

"What are you having?" Joe asked.

Chet rolled his eyes. "Anything but pizza," he said. "See you tomorrow."

* * *

9

That night, after a meat-loaf dinner, the Hardys worked on their homework. It was hard not to think about pizzas.

"I know," Frank said. He pointed to his space science book. "A Cosmic Pie with Crusty Craters."

Joe held up his dinosaur book. "How about a Colossal-Fossil Pie?"

Frank shut his book. "I have a better idea. Let's call it a night."

The boys went to bed. But Joe couldn't sleep. All he could think about were pizzas, pizzas, and more pizzas.

"Banana-split pizza . . . spaghetti pizza . . . s'mores pizza . . . ZZZZZZZ."

Joe finally fell asleep. He woke up a few hours later when his dad knocked on the door.

"Joe, Chet is on the phone," Mr. Hardy called. "He says it's an emergency!"

2

Dreams and Schemes

Joe ran into his parents' bedroom. Frank was already there with the phone in his hand.

"Chet? Are you okay?" Frank asked into the phone.

"Sure," Chet answered. "Why not?"

Frank looked at the clock. "Because it's three o'clock in the morning."

"Oh, yeah," Chet said. "I just wanted to tell you about this crazy dream I had."

"You woke up my family for a stupid dream?" Frank hissed into the phone.

11

"Tell Chet it can wait until tomorrow," Mrs. Hardy said sleepily.

"Chet—" Frank began to say.

"I dreamed about a *pizza!*" Chet said.

Frank covered the receiver. He turned to Joe. "He says he dreamed about a pizza."

"Was it chasing him?" Joe asked.

"Listen, you guys," Chet begged over the phone. "It wasn't just any pizza. It was the perfect pizza. For the contest!"

Frank turned to Joe. "He dreamed about the perfect pizza for the contest."

"Cool," Joe said.

"It's so awesome, my mouth was watering in my sleep," Chet said. "My pillow was soaking wet!"

"Boys," Mr. Hardy said. "This isn't the time for a Chet-chat."

"In a second, Dad," Joe said.

"Chet," Frank said. "Write down the recipe. Then meet us at the supermarket tomorrow morning at ten o'clock."

"What for?" Chet asked.

"So we can pick up stuff for your dream pizza," Frank explained.

"Great," Chet said. "I'll ask my dad to drop me off."

"Boys!" Mr. Hardy warned.

"Gotta go," Frank told Chet. "Remember. Write down everything. To the last meatball."

"Meatball?" Chet asked. "My pizza is much more exciting than that. I laugh at meatballs!"

"Goodbye, Chet," Frank said. He hung up with a click.

Frank and Joe walked back to their rooms.

"Leave it to Chet to dream about food," Frank said with a smile.

"What else is new?" Joe said. "He counts lamb chops instead of sheep."

Saturday morning after breakfast Mrs. Hardy drove the boys to the Ripe Apple Supermarket. Chet was waiting for them outside by the row of gumball machines.

"Here it is," Chet said. He waved a piece of paper in the air. "The Chet Morton Dream Pizza!"

"Cool!" Joe said.

"Show us when we get inside," Frank suggested. "My mom wants to get started."

The boys followed Mrs. Hardy through the automatic doors. Joe looked around the supermarket. Then he saw someone he knew.

"There's Kevin," Joe said.

Kevin was wheeling a shopping cart. He was with his dad.

"Hi, Kevin," Frank called. "Hi, Mr. Saris."

Mr. Saris smiled and waved. But Kevin didn't. He looked straight ahead as he pushed the cart.

"Uh-oh," Joe said. "It looks like Kevin is mad at us."

Frank shrugged. "He didn't say we shouldn't enter the contest," he said.

Mrs. Hardy wheeled over an empty shopping cart. "You boys can use your own cart for your pizza ingredients," she said.

"Thanks, Mom," Frank said.

Mrs. Hardy looked at her watch. "We'll meet at the checkout line in forty minutes," she said.

"Don't you guys want to see my pizza recipe?" Chet asked after Mrs. Hardy left.

"Let's find the contest display first," Frank said.

"And pick up the rules," Joe added.

The contest display was in front of the frozen-foods section. A stack of rules and a sign-in sheet were stapled to the front.

Frank was about to reach for the rules when a boy with brown hair and a purple backpack came over.

"What's up?" the boy asked.

Chet smiled at the boy. "Aren't you Carl? From the fifth grade?" he asked.

"Yeah, but you probably know me from all the school plays I've been in,"

Carl said. He began counting on his fingers. *"Jack in the Beanstalk . . . Pinocchio—"*

Frank wanted to change the subject. "Are you entering this contest, too?" he asked Carl.

Carl shook his head. "My mom's shopping. Then she's dropping me off at school for a dress rehearsal."

"You're in *another* school play?" Joe asked.

"I'm the *star* of *Peter Pan*," Carl said proudly.

"Oh, yeah?" Chet asked. "What part?"

"Du-uh!" Carl said. "I'm Peter Pan."

"In that case," Chet joked, "the peanut butter is in aisle three. Ha! Ha!"

"Yuk, yuk," Carl muttered.

Frank, Joe, and Chet wrote their names on the contest sign-in list. Then they each tore off a sheet of rules.

Joe gazed at the colorful picture of the superheroes. "I really want to be on the

16

Pumped-Up Power Patrol show," he said.

"Me, too," Carl said. "If I was on TV, the whole country would see what a great actor I am."

"Oh, brother," Chet muttered.

"Then why don't you enter the contest?" Frank asked.

"And come up with a stupid pizza recipe?" Carl asked.

"Our pizza isn't stupid," Chet said. He waved the recipe in Carl's face. "It's a sure winner."

"A winner, huh?" Carl said. He stared at the recipe. "Can I be on your team?"

"You just called the contest stupid," Frank protested.

"It *is* stupid," Carl said. "But the prize isn't."

"Sorry, Carl—" Frank began to say.

"Come on, you guys," Carl begged. "How else will I get to Hollywood?"

Chet dropped his dream recipe in the

empty cart. "You're Peter Pan," he said. "Why don't you *fly*?"

Just then a voice came over the loudspeaker. "Attention, shoppers!" it said. "Pick up free cookie samples in aisle five."

"Cookies?" Chet cried. He began to run. "I'm there!"

Frank and Joe ran after Chet. But as they ran up aisle five, Frank stopped.

"Wait, you guys," he said. "We left the shopping cart alone."

"And my recipe!" Chet said.

The boys spun around and raced back to the shopping cart. They stared into it. It was empty except for an unfamiliar hunk of white cheese.

"Uh-oh," Joe said with a gulp.

"My dream pizza recipe," Chet said. His voice cracked. "It's gone!"

3

Clue? Pe-ew!

"Maybe the recipe fell through the shopping cart," Joe said.

The boys dropped down on their hands and knees. They searched under the cart.

"It's not under here," Frank said. "Someone must have taken it."

Joe looked into the cart again. He picked up the cheese.

"How did this get in here?" he asked.

"I don't know," Frank said. He grabbed his nose. "But it sure stinks."

"Let's go up and down the aisles," Joe said. He dropped the cheese back in the cart. "The person who took the recipe might still be holding it."

The boys ran toward aisle one. They skidded around the corner.

Frank saw a woman walking toward them with an armload of cereal boxes.

"Look out!" he shouted.

It was too late. Frank, Joe, and Chet crashed into the woman. The cereal boxes tumbled to the floor.

"Sorry," the boys mumbled. They looked down as they knelt to pick up the boxes.

"Hello, boys," said a voice.

The boys glanced up and gasped. It was their principal, Ms. Vaughn!

"H-hello, Ms. Vaughn," Frank said.

"Nice . . . running into you," Chet said.

"What were you doing running in the supermarket?" Ms. Vaughn asked.

"You've heard of the express lane, Ms. Vaughn?" Chet asked quickly.

Ms. Vaughn nodded.

"Well, we thought this was the *express aisle*," Chet said.

"Oh, brother," Joe mumbled.

"From now on walk slowly," Ms. Vaughn said. "Just as we do in school."

"Yes, Ms. Vaughn," Joe said. "Bye, Ms. Vaughn."

The boys looked over their shoulders as they walked back to the shopping cart.

"Hey," Chet said. "I just figured out something awesome."

"About the missing recipe?" Joe asked.

"No, about Ms. Vaughn," Chet said. "She eats Flakey Wakeys—and so do I."

Frank gave a big sigh. "Let's start looking for clues," he said.

Joe pointed to the hunk of cheese. "Is that a clue?" he asked.

"Nah," Frank said. "Just the stinkiest thing I ever smelled in my life."

"Oh, yeah?" Joe said. "Try your sneakers after a basketball game. Pe-eeww!"

Frank flipped the cheese over. He read the label. "This cheese is called Limburger," he said.

"Carl!" Chet gasped.

"Carl eats this stuff?" Joe asked.

"No," Chet said. "Carl's last name is Limburger."

Frank gave it a thought. "I wonder if this cheese was a sign from Carl."

"A sign?" Joe asked.

"Carl wanted to enter the contest, but he didn't want to come up with a pizza idea," Frank said. "He just wanted to win."

Joe snapped his fingers. "So he might have taken the recipe and left the cheese."

Chet slapped his forehead. "And I told him that we had a prizewinning recipe. Stupid! Stupid! Stupid!"

"Easy, Chet," Frank said. "We don't know if Carl even entered the contest."

"And if we don't find the recipe, you probably still remember it," Joe said.

Chet gulped. "Oh, yeah?"

"Chet," Joe repeated. "You do remember it, don't you?"

"I never remember my dreams," Chet said. "Not even my nightmares!"

Frank grabbed Chet by the shoulders. He shook him lightly. "Chet," he said. "Think hard. What was on that pizza?"

Chet screwed up his face. Frank and Joe saw that he was really thinking. Finally Chet spoke:

"Marshmallows?" he asked.

"On a pizza?" Joe cried.

Chet explained. "When I try to remember, I see a blank space. Like a movie screen before the movie comes on."

Frank pushed the shopping cart. "Try your best to remember," he told Chet.

The boys went through the supermarket. Frank grabbed a package of instant pizza crust. Chet walked as if he were in a trance. He called out items one by one.

25

"Licorice . . . sardines . . . baked beans . . ."

After they filled up the cart, Frank and Joe stared into it.

"I think I'm going to barf," Joe said slowly.

"Okay, okay," Chet said. He picked up a package of pickled pig's feet. "We can make this work."

Just then there was a loud ripping noise. Frank and Joe turned to see a teenage boy ripping open a box. He wore a red Ripe Apple smock.

"That's Zack Jackson's brother, Tim," Frank whispered. "I guess he works here."

"He doesn't look like Zack," Joe said.

"You guys don't look like brothers, either," Chet told Frank and Joe.

Chet was right. Frank had brown hair and brown eyes. Joe had blond hair and blue eyes.

"You guys," Joe said. "Maybe Tim stole the recipe for Zack!"

"We don't know for sure if the Zack Pack entered the contest," Frank said.

"Zack probably made it up to tease us," Chet said.

"I know," Joe said. "Let's check out the sign-in sheet."

Frank, Joe, and Chet wheeled their cart back to the contest display.

"There's Zack's name," Frank said. He pointed to the sign-in sheet. "And Mark's and Brett's."

"Uh-oh," Joe said. "Look who else entered the contest."

"Who?" Chet asked.

"The 'big cheese' himself," Joe said. "Carl Limburger."

4

Backpack Attack

Carl must have stolen my recipe," Chet insisted. "And stuffed it in his backpack."

"We don't know that for sure," Frank said.

"Let's ask Mom to drop us off at school later," Joe said.

"School?" Chet cried. "On Saturday?"

"Carl said he was rehearsing *Peter Pan* at school today," Joe explained. "Maybe we can check him out—and his backpack."

Chet gave a big sigh. "First we run into

Ms. Vaughn. Then we go to school," he said. "It might as well be Monday!"

After paying for the groceries, Mrs. Hardy dropped the boys off at their school.

Joe patted his jacket pocket. "I have the Limburger cheese," he said. "In case we need it to question Carl."

Chet squeezed his nose. "That stuff will make anybody confess."

The boys walked through the schoolyard. Chet's sister, Iola, was tossing a Frisbee with her friends Keisha Green and Tammy Sung.

"Hi, guys," Iola called. "Are you entering the pizza contest?"

"You bet," Chet said.

Iola smiled. "Then get ready for some major competition," she said.

Tammy nodded. "We're entering the pizza contest, too," she said.

"What do you know about pizza, Iola?" Chet asked. "You eat your slice with a knife and fork. That's no way to eat pizza."

"At least I'm not a slob," Iola said.

Tammy put her arm around Keisha's shoulder. "We're going to win because we have Keisha on our team," she said.

"Is Keisha a good cook?" Frank asked.

"Nope," Iola said. "But she *is* the best artist in the school."

Chet groaned. "The Power Patrol is going to *taste* the pizzas, not hang them on their walls," he said.

"You'll see," Iola said. "Our pizza is going to be a masterpiece."

"You mean a—master-pizza!" Joe said with a laugh.

"You won't be laughing when we win," Iola called as the boys walked toward the school.

"Blah, blah, blah!" Chet called back.

"I'll bet the rehearsal is in the auditorium," Frank said when they reached the building.

"I was in a play once," Chet said. "We kept our backpacks and jackets backstage."

Joe snapped his fingers. "There's a side door that leads right into the auditorium," he said.

"Let's go," Frank said.

They ran to the door. But it was locked.

"I guess we'll have to use the back door to the auditorium," Frank said.

The boys entered the school through the main door. Then they ran down the hall to the auditorium. They opened the back door a crack so they could see inside.

"There's Carl," Frank whispered. "And the drama teacher, Mr. Korman."

Carl was wearing his green Peter Pan costume. He ran across the stage and flapped his arms up and down.

" 'I'm flyyyyying!' " Carl sang.

"More energy!" Mr. Korman shouted.

Carl looked over his shoulder. Then he

slammed right into a cardboard tree. His feathered cap flew off his head.

"Ow!" Carl cried. He rubbed his nose. "Why do I have to fly anyway, Mr. Korman?"

"Because you're Peter Pan," Mr. Korman declared. "Tinker Bell never complains."

Frank turned to Chet and Joe. "We have to figure out how to get backstage without them seeing us," he said.

"But how?" Joe asked.

Frank looked around. He saw a costume rack at the end of the hall.

"We can sneak backstage wearing those costumes," Frank said. "Mr. Korman and Carl will think we're in the play."

"We'll be like undercover detectives!" Joe cried.

The boys ran to the rack. There were three costumes hanging on it.

"I'll be Mr. Smee, the pirate," Frank

whispered. He grabbed a striped shirt and dark pants.

"Cool!" Chet said. He grabbed a purple jacket and big feathered hat. "I want to be Captain Hook."

Chet pulled the black eyepatch over his eye. "Arrrgh! Walk the plank, Limburgaaaargh!" he snarled.

"Shhhh!" Frank warned.

Joe reached for the last costume. "I guess that leaves me with . . ."

He stared at the costume and shrieked.

"Tiger Lily?" Joe said with a gulp. He picked up the long braided wig. "No way!"

Frank laughed. "I thought you wanted to be an undercover detective."

The boys pulled their costumes on over their clothes.

"Remember," Frank said in a low voice. He adjusted his cap. "When we walk through the auditorium, keep your heads low."

"Gotcha," Joe said. His braids bobbed as he nodded.

The boys opened the back door. They walked quickly through the auditorium.

"Wait backstage until we practice your scenes, kids," Mr. Korman called.

Joe could see Carl staring at him.

"Since when does Tiger Lily wear high-tops?" Carl asked Mr. Korman.

Frank, Joe, and Chet ran through the curtain. They were finally backstage.

Chet raised his hand. "High five!"

"Watch that hook, Chet!" Joe cried.

"Quick. Let's look for Carl's backpack," Frank said in a low voice.

Joe glanced around. He saw a big cardboard pirate ship and a model of Skull Rock. Then he saw a purple backpack leaning against a coil of ropes.

"Carl's backpack," he said.

"There's a piece of paper sticking out of the front pocket," Frank said.

"I'll bet it's my pizza recipe," Chet said.

The boys hurried over to the back-pack. Frank pulled up the paper.

"Forget it," Frank said. "It's the rules for the Power Patrol contest."

"I'll bet my recipe is *inside* the back-pack," Chet said. He reached for the zipper.

Just then Frank heard the sound of footsteps. "Someone's coming," he hissed.

The Hardys ran for the side door.

"Wait!" Chet called. "My hook is caught on Carl's backpack."

Three kids burst through the curtain. The Hardys and Chet froze.

"They're wearing our costumes!" a girl with glasses cried.

A fourth-grade boy pointed to the backpack hanging from Chet's hook-hand.

"And they're stealing our backpacks!" he shouted.

5

Recipe for Trouble

What's going on back here?" Mr. Korman asked as he ran backstage with Carl.

"Let go of my backpack!" Carl shouted at Chet.

"I can't!" Chet said.

Carl marched up to Chet. He lifted his eyepatch. "Morton? Is that you?" he asked.

Chet nodded. Then Carl turned to Frank and Joe.

"Frank?" he asked. He looked at Joe and laughed. "Joe?"

37

Joe tugged at his Tiger Lily dress. "Yeah, yeah," he muttered.

Mr. Korman folded his arms across his chest. "I think you boys have some explaining to do," he said.

"So does Carl," Joe said quickly.

"Why me?" Carl asked.

Joe reached into his pocket and pulled out the stinky cheese. The kids gasped and jumped back.

"How do you explain *this*, Mr. *Limburger?*" Joe asked. He held the cheese in front of Carl's nose.

"What is going on here?" Mr. Korman demanded.

Frank turned to Mr. Korman. He explained about the missing recipe.

"Why would I want to steal your pizza idea?" Carl asked.

"Because you didn't want to come up with your own," Joe said.

"But I did come up with a pizza idea," Carl said. "A *great* pizza idea."

"You did?" Chet asked.

Carl nodded. "It's called the Carl Goes Hollywood Pizza."

"Carl Goes Hollywood?" Joe asked.

Carl nodded. "In the middle will be a big star made of cheese," he said. "And my name will be written on it with pepperoni and mushrooms."

"Fabulous!" Mr. Korman said.

"Sick," Chet mumbled.

"So I don't need your stupid pizza recipe," Carl told the boys.

"Good," Joe said. He yanked off the Tiger Lily wig. "Then we don't need your costumes."

The boys returned the costumes. Then they left the school.

"So Carl's off the hook," Joe said as they walked through the schoolyard.

"Did you have to say *hook*?" Chet groaned.

Joe looked around the schoolyard. Iola and her friends were not there. In their place was the Zack Pack.

"Oh, great," Joe said. "Another Zack attack."

Zack, Brett, and Mark were riding their bikes in circles around a squirrel. When they saw the Hardys and Chet, they rode their bikes toward them.

"Ring around the losers!" Zack sang as they circled around the boys.

Joe pretended to yawn. "We're really worried," he said.

"I'd worry about the pizza contest if I were you," Zack called from his bike.

"Yeah!" Brett shouted. "We just got the best pizza recipe in the whole world."

"So give up now!" Zack shouted.

"Give up now! Give up now!" the Zack Pack chanted together as they zoomed away.

"Zack's brother probably gave them our recipe already," Frank said.

"My brilliant recipe," Chet wailed. "In the hands of jerks!"

"Let's follow the Zack Pack," Joe suggested.

Frank shook his head. "The contest is tomorrow. If we still want to enter, we have to start working on our pizza."

"You mean that gross thing Chet came up with in the supermarket?" Joe asked.

"Hey!" Chet complained.

Frank shrugged. "It's better than nothing. Besides, maybe the Pumped-Up Power Patrol likes licorice and sardines."

"Let's make the pizza in your kitchen," Chet said. "I don't want Iola and her friends to see what we're doing."

"Yeah," Joe agreed. "The last thing we need is spies."

When the boys reached the Hardys' house, they cleared the kitchen for their pizza project. Then they laid out all of the ingredients.

"Where do we start?" Joe asked.

Frank picked up a package of Trusty

Crusty. "All pizzas start with the crust," he said.

"How do we make it?" Joe asked.

"It's instant," Frank said. "We just dump it, roll it, and bake it."

Frank cut open the package. He plopped the heavy lump of dough on the counter.

Joe grabbed a wooden rolling pin. "Let's make it nice and flat," he said.

The boys took turns rolling the pin back and forth over the dough. Finally they had a nice flat circle.

Joe touched it. "It feels sticky. Are you sure it doesn't need anything?"

"We have to flip it," Chet suggested.

"Flip it?" Frank asked.

"Like they do at Pizza Paradise," Chet said. "Kevin's dad flips the pizza dough up and down in the air all the time."

"Who's going to flip it?" Frank asked.

"I will," Chet said. "I'm the best Frisbee catcher in Bayport."

Frank and Joe stared at Chet.

"Frisbees . . . dough . . . same thing," Chet said. He carefully reached under the dough. He lifted it in both hands.

"One, two," Chet counted. Then he hurled the dough over his head. "Three!"

The boys stared up. Seconds passed.

"Why didn't it come down?" Joe asked.

"Because it's stuck on the ceiling, that's why," Frank said.

Chet shook his head. "This never happens with Frisbees."

Suddenly the dough began to sag.

"Look out below!" Joe shouted.

The pizza dough fell from the ceiling. It landed over Chet's head and shoulders with a loud splat.

"Ahhhh!" Chet screamed under the dough. "It's going to eat me alive!"

"I'll help you," Joe said. He tore two holes in the dough for Chet's eyes.

There was a rap on the kitchen door.

"Who's that?" Joe asked.

Frank went to the door. He opened it.

No one was there. But just as he was about to go back inside, he saw something on the ground.

"It's a pizza box," Frank said.

Chet ripped the dough off his head. He tossed it on the counter. "Did you say pizza?" he asked.

"What kind is it?" Joe asked.

Frank peeked inside the box.

"The kind you don't want," he said. He held up the pizza.

Written in black olives was a message. It read: "Give up now!"

6

Last Chance Trance

The Zack Pack told us to give up in the schoolyard," Joe said. "I'll bet this pizza's from them."

"Don't forget what Dad always says," Frank told Joe. "Consider all possible suspects."

"But who else is there?" Joe asked.

Frank closed the lid. "This pie is from Pizza Paradise," he said slowly.

"Kevin's parents own Pizza Paradise," Chet said.

Joe stared at the box. "You don't think Kevin sent the pizza, do you?"

"Kevin seemed mad at us for entering the contest," Frank said.

"Hey, wait a minute," Chet said. "He was also in the supermarket this morning."

Joe shook his head. "Kevin can't be a suspect. He's our friend."

"We don't know who stole the recipe," Frank said. "Or sent this message. But this pizza is a great clue."

"And a tasty one," Chet said. He reached into the box and picked up a slice.

"Chet!" Joe shouted. "You're eating the evidence."

Chet took a bite and swallowed. "Since when do we waste a great pizza?" he asked.

"I think we should finish baking our own pizza first," Frank insisted.

The boys flattened out the dough again. They dumped all of the ingredients on top. Then they called Mrs. Hardy to put it in the oven.

"Your pizza should be ready in about half an hour," Mrs. Hardy said.

"What do we do in the meantime?" Joe asked Frank and Chet.

Frank looked at the clock. "We can watch *People Are Strange* on TV."

The boys carried the Pizza Paradise pizza and paper plates to the den. Then they turned on the TV.

"Welcome to *People Are Strange*. I'm your host, Bob Oddly," the man on TV said. "Our guest today is Dr. Sigmund Von Trance, the world-famous hypnotist."

Joe picked up a slice of pizza. "Cool," he said.

"Who are you hypnotizing today, Dr. Von Trance?" Bob asked the doctor.

The gray-haired doctor pointed to a man sitting on a stool. "Today I will make Mr. Rizzo think he is a pussycat."

"Fat chance!" Mr. Rizzo laughed.

The doctor went on. "The only way

Mr. Rizzo can come out of the trance is if I clap my hands three times."

Dr. Von Trance swung a pendant in front of Mr. Rizzo's face for about half a minute.

"When I count to three, you will be a tabby named Fluffy," he told Mr. Rizzo. "One . . . two . . . three."

"Meooooowww!" Mr. Rizzo howled. Then he licked both his hands.

"Wow!" Frank said.

"I hope his house has a litter box," Chet said. He popped an olive in his mouth.

The audience clapped as Mr. Rizzo chased a windup mouse around the set.

"What else can you make people do, Dr. Von Trance?" Bob Oddly asked.

"I can make people remember just about anything," Dr. Von Trance said.

Joe laughed. "Maybe he can get Chet to remember his dream pizza," he said.

Frank stopped eating his slice. "That's it!" he cried.

"What?" Joe asked.

"Mike Mendez invented some kind of gadget that's supposed to hypnotize people," Frank said.

Mike Mendez was the Hardys' friend. He was always inventing things.

"Do you think Mike can hypnotize Chet?" Joe asked Frank.

"It's worth a shot," Frank said.

Chet waved his hands in the air. "Hello? Remember me? I didn't say I wanted to be hypnotized," he said.

"It'll be a blast, Chet," Joe said.

Chet pointed to Mr. Rizzo on the TV screen. "You call chasing mice and hacking up fur balls a blast?"

Dr. Von Trance clapped his hands three times. Mr. Rizzo stopped chasing the mouse. "What happened?" Mr. Rizzo asked.

"See?" Joe said. "He's fine."

"Yeah, but—" Chet began to say.

"Your pizza is ready, guys!" Mrs. Hardy called from the kitchen.

The boys ran into the kitchen. Frank put on two oven mitts. He carefully pulled the pizza out. The crusty pie oozed with peanut butter, cottage cheese, salami, sauerkraut, and other things.

Chet stared at the pizza. "We forgot the jelly beans," he said.

"Why don't we just forget this whole pie," Joe asked. "It looks disgusting."

"There goes our chance to be on the *Pumped-Up Power Patrol* show," Frank said.

"Okay, I'll do it," Chet said quickly.

"Do what?" Frank asked.

"I'll be hynotized," Chet said. "I want to be on the show as much as you do."

"Thanks, Chet!" Joe said.

Frank dialed Mike's number. Chet took the phone and explained everything.

"Great," Mike said over the phone. "I've always wanted to try out my Hypno-Helmet."

"You've never tried it out before?"

Chet asked. He groaned. "I feel like a lab rat!"

The next morning the Hardys and Chet rode their bikes to the Mendezes' house.

"What's that smell?" Mike asked as they went into his room.

Joe patted his pocket. "I guess I forgot to take the Limburger cheese out of my jacket yesterday," he said.

"It smells even worse today," Frank complained.

Mike picked up a football helmet with a yo-yo tied to the front. "Ta-daaa!" he sang.

"What's with the yo-yo?" Joe asked.

"When it swings back and forth, it'll put Chet in a trance," Mike explained.

"Gee. I can't wait," Chet mumbled. He sat down on a chair. Mike placed the helmet over his head.

"Do I have to watch this thing?" Chet

asked as the yo-yo swung back and forth. "It's making me dizzy."

"Definitely," Mike said.

Chet watched the swinging yo-yo for a few seconds.

"You are totally relaxed," Mike said. "Your eyelids feel very, very heavy."

Chet's eyes crossed. Then they closed.

"His dream," Joe whispered. "Make him remember his dream."

"You begin to remember your dream," Mike said to Chet.

"My dream . . . my dream," Chet mumbled. His eyes popped wide open. Then he yanked off the helmet and stood up.

"BRAAAWP! BRAAAWP!" Chet croaked.

"What was that?" Frank asked.

"It sounded like a frog," Mike said.

Chet flicked out his tongue. He rolled his eyes and jumped around the room.

"BRAAAWP! BRAAAWP!"

"Oh, no!" Joe said. "Chet must have dreamed about frogs last night."

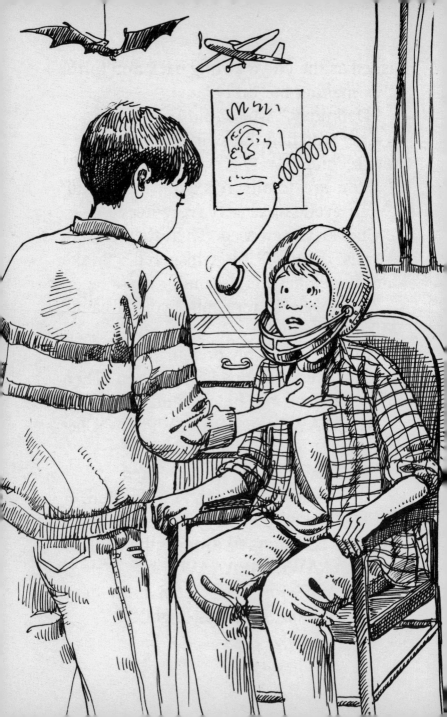

"He dreamed about the pizza on *Friday* night," Frank said.

"Now you tell me," Mike groaned.

Chet leaped around Mike's room. He pulled books off shelves. He knocked over Mike's experiments. Frank and Joe tried to stop Chet, but he was too fast.

"He's trashing my room!" Mike shouted.

Chet dug his fist into a plastic jar.

"My rubber insect collection," Mike said. "What does he want with it?"

Joe shrugged. "Frogs love bugs."

Chet grabbed a handful of creepy crawlies. He brought them to his mouth.

"Don't eat them, Chet!" Frank called.

Chet croaked again. He shoved the rubber bugs into his pants pocket.

"Don't you know how to bring him out of the trance?" Joe asked Mike.

"Not really," Mike said.

Frank and Joe stared at Mike. "What?" they asked.

7

Run for Your Life!

BRAAAWP!" Chet croaked. He jumped up and down on Mike's bed. "BRAAWP!"

"What did Dr. Von Trance do on TV?" Joe asked Frank.

"He clapped his hands three times," Frank said.

Frank quickly clapped his hands. Chet stopped jumping. He blinked his eyes.

"What am I doing on your bed?" Chet asked Mike.

"You were hypnotized," Mike said. "You thought you were a frog."

"A frog who remembered the pizza recipe?" Chet asked hopefully.

"Nah," Joe said. "Just a frog."

"Bummer," Chet said. "Let's try it again."

"And mess up my room even more?" Mike said. "No way."

After helping Mike clean his room, Frank, Joe, and Chet left the Mendez house.

"I guess we can forget about my pizza recipe," Chet said with a sigh.

"Not really," Frank said. "We still have two suspects to check out."

"The contest is in a few hours," Chet said. "Even if we find the recipe, we'll never have enough time to bake the pizza."

"I know," Frank said. "But maybe we can stop the thief from entering the contest, too."

"Which suspect do we check out first," Chet asked. "Zack or Kevin?"

"Zack," Joe said quickly. "His house is just two blocks from here."

The boys rode their bikes to Zack's block.

"Uh-oh," Joe called from his bike. "Look who's going into Zack's house. Mark and Brett."

"They're carrying groceries," Chet said. "What if they're about to bake my pizza?"

Frank smiled. "Then we'll catch them in the act," he said.

The boys waited until Mark and Brett were inside. They got off their bikes and walked quietly to the house.

"There's an open window," Frank whispered. "Let's look inside."

The boys crouched under the window. They raised their heads and peeked in.

"They're in the kitchen," Frank whispered.

Zack, Mark, and Brett were leaning over the kitchen counter.

"It looks like they're reading something," Joe whispered.

Frank and Joe strained their ears to listen.

"Do you think the Power Patrol will know we stole this pizza recipe?" Mark asked Zack.

"Who cares?" Zack sneered.

Chet grabbed Frank's arm. "That's probably my recipe they're talking about," he whispered. "Let's fight 'em for it."

"Fight the Zack Pack?" Joe said. "They're some of the biggest guys in the whole school."

Zack began to sniff the air.

"What's that smell?" he asked.

Joe bit his lip. "The Limburger cheese," he whispered. But it was too late.

Mark looked up at the window. "Spies!" he yelled.

"Let's get 'em!" Brett said.

Chet groaned. "Busted!"

Frank turned to Joe and Chet. "Run for your life!" he ordered.

They raced toward their bikes. The Zack Pack was close behind. Brett waved a heavy book in the air.

"You and that stupid cheese," Chet told Joe as they ran.

The bullies caught up with the Hardys and Chet. They backed them against a tree.

"Gotcha," Zack sneered.

"Oh, yeah?" Joe asked. He reached into his pocket and pulled out the cheese. The Zack Pack jumped back.

"Ugh!" Zack shouted. "Get it away."

"Not until you return our pizza recipe," Frank said.

"*Your* pizza recipe?" Zack asked. "None of you is Chef Gorgonzola."

"Who's Chef Gorgonzola?" Joe asked.

Brett picked up his book. The cover read *100 Creative Pizza Ideas by Chef Gorgonzola.*

"So that's where you stole your pizza idea from," Frank said. "A cookbook."

"What's the big deal?" Zack asked.

"It's against the contest rules," Joe said. "You should drop out of the contest."

"And *you* should mind your own business!" Zack shouted.

"Knock it off, Zack," came a gruff voice. A teenage boy stepped out from behind a tree. It was Zack's brother, Tim.

"I heard everything," Tim told Zack. "Forget about the book and think up your own recipe. Just as the rules say."

"What if I don't?" Zack asked.

"Then I'll take my old TV back," Tim said. "And you'll never watch *Power Patrol* in your room again."

Zack's face froze. "I love that TV," he muttered. He turned to Mark and Brett. "Come on. Let's cook up something else."

"But, Zack—" Brett began to say.

"I said, let's cook up something else!"

Zack shouted. He stomped back to the house. Mark and Brett followed.

"Hey, you guys," Frank called. "Did you leave that pizza box in front of our door last night?"

"What pizza box?" Zack growled.

"What are you taking about?" Mark asked.

Joe sighed. "I guess we have only one suspect left—Kevin Saris."

"Wait," Frank said. He took the cheese from Joe and tossed it to Tim.

"You work in the supermarket," Frank said. "Who buys this kind of cheese?"

Tim made a face. "I know only one person who asks for this," he said.

"Who?" Frank asked excitedly.

"The principal of Bayport Elementary School," Tim said. "Ms. Vaughn."

8

And the Winner Is . . .

Ms. Vaughn?" Joe repeated as Tim walked back to the house.

"Ms. Vaughn was in the supermarket yesterday, too," Frank said.

"Why would Ms. Vaughn want to steal my recipe?" Chet asked.

Frank thought for a while. "Doesn't Ms. Vaughn live on Gull Street?" he asked.

Joe nodded. "That's four blocks from here," he said.

"Let's see what we can find out,"

Frank suggested. The boys rode their bikes the few blocks to Gull Street.

"Which house is Ms. Vaughn's?" Frank asked.

Joe pointed. "It's probably the one with all the teachers going into it."

Ms. Vaughn was standing on the doorstep of a yellow house. She waved as teachers from Bayport Elementary stepped up to the door.

Chet shook his head. "Teachers on a Sunday," he said. "Too weird."

Ms. Vaughn was about to close the door when she turned toward the boys.

"Hi, boys!" she called.

The boys walked over to Ms. Vaughn.

"Hello, Ms. Vaughn," Frank said.

"Are you having some kind of party today?" Chet asked.

Ms. Vaughn nodded. "It's my annual Sunday teachers' brunch. And I just baked the perfect pizza pie."

The boys stared at Ms. Vaughn.

"Y-y-you what?" Joe stammered.

Ms. Vaughn pulled a piece of paper from her pocket. "I found this recipe lying in my shopping cart yesterday."

"My dream pizza!" Chet gasped.

"Of course, my Limburger cheese was missing," Ms. Vaughn said. "But I can't really remember if I put that in."

Joe yanked the cheese from his jacket pocket. "Is this it?" he asked quickly.

"Why, yes," Ms. Vaughn said.

Frank thought for a moment. Then he turned to Chet and Joe.

"Our carts were switched," he said.

"Excuse me?" Ms. Vaughn asked.

"That pizza recipe was in *our* shopping cart," Frank said. "And the cheese was in yours."

Ms. Vaughn looked confused.

"Did you leave your pizza cart alone at any time, Ms. Vaughn?" Joe asked.

Ms. Vaughn thought for a while.

"Only when I went to the frozen section," she said.

Joe turned to Frank and Chet. "That's where the contest display was," he said.

"And that's where we left our cart when we ran for the cookies," Chet said.

Ms. Vaughn put her hands on her hips. "Hmm," she said. "Was this another case for the Clues Brothers?"

Frank took a deep breath. Then he told Ms. Vaughn everything about the contest and the missing recipe.

"I see," Ms. Vaughn said slowly. "So when I went back to my cart, I took yours instead. I'm sorry."

Frank looked at his watch. "It's okay. We can still make the contest," he said.

Joe quickly handed Ms. Vaughn the cheese. "Here's your cheese. Now all we need is the pizza pie," he said.

Ms. Vaughn shook her head. "I can't give you that pizza. What else will I feed the teachers?" she asked.

"Let them eat Limburger!" Chet cried.

Ms. Vaughn handed Chet his recipe.

"Maybe you can bake a new pizza for the contest," she said.

Frank and Joe looked at each other. They knew there wasn't enough time.

"Ms. Vaughn?" Joe asked. "Can we at least see how the pizza came out?"

Ms. Vaughn opened the door wide. "Sure," she said. "Come on in."

The boys followed Ms. Vaughn to the dining room. The teachers from Bayport Elementary School were standing around, eating fruit salad.

"There it is!" Chet said. He pointed to a table against a wall. A large pizza stood in the middle. "My dream pizza!"

Chet ran to the table.

"At least the case is solved," Joe said to Frank. "But we still don't know who left that weird message at our door yesterday."

"The only person I can think of is Kevin," Frank said.

Frank and Joe joined Chet at the table. Chet began to sniffle.

"Chet?" Frank asked. "What's wrong?"

"My dream pizza is so . . . beautiful." Chet sniffed. "I need my hankie."

Chet reached into his pocket. "Hey, what's this?" he asked. He pulled out Mike's rubber bugs. Some of the bugs dropped on the pizza.

"Watch it, Chet," Frank said. "You're getting creepy crawlies all over the pie."

But just as the boys were about to pick them off, Ms. Pell, the girls' gym teacher, came over.

"Oh, my goodness," she said. "There are bugs on that pizza!"

Ms. Goldberg, the school librarian, looked over Ms. Pell's shoulder. "Those look like rare bugs from the forests of Central America. The poisonous kind!"

The teachers gasped. Ms. Vaughn ran over. "What do you mean, bugs?" she asked.

Joe stared at the teachers. Then he stared at the pizza. He had an idea.

"Don't worry, everybody!" Joe shouted. "We'll get this nasty thing out of here!"

The teachers jumped back as Frank grabbed the pizza off the table.

"Stand back," Frank said. "They can be real party animals!"

"Insects," Ms. Goldberg corrected.

The boys ran out of the house and to their bikes. Frank plopped the pizza on top of his bicycle basket.

"We can still make the contest if we hurry," Frank said.

The three boys raced their bikes to the Bayport Mall. They locked them to a bicycle rack and ran inside.

A big crowd stood in front of a long table filled with pizza pies.

"There's the Pumped-Up Power Patrol!" Joe cried. He pointed to four guys in silver jumpsuits and helmets.

"It looks like they're tasting the last pizza," Chet said.

"Wait!" Frank shouted. He ran to the table. "Here's one more."

"Don't swallow the bugs," Chet called.

Frank, Joe, and Chet watched as the Power Patrol tasted their pizza.

"Not bad," Pumped-Up Pablo said.

Joe gave a thumbs-up sign. "Ye-es!" he said.

Everyone was silent as the four superheroes looked over the pizzas. Then they turned to the crowd.

"The winners are Iola, Keisha, and Tammy!" Pumped-Up Pete shouted. "For their pizza-portrait of George Washington."

"George Washington?" Joe cried.

Pumped-Up Pierre held up the winning pie. George Washington's face was made out of mozzarella cheese. His hair was sausage, and his eyes and mouth were mushrooms.

"Arrrgh!" Chet groaned. "I can't believe we lost to my sister."

Iola and her friends jumped up and down and cheered.

"Well, at least the Zack Pack didn't

enter," Frank said, looking around. "They must have given up."

"Let's go," Chet said. "I need an emergency pickle on a stick."

The boys slowly turned around. They saw Kevin standing behind them.

"Hi, guys," Kevin said with a smile.

"What are you doing here?" Joe asked.

Kevin picked up a notebook. "I'm writing about the contest for the school paper," he said.

"We thought you hated this contest," Joe said.

"Not anymore," Kevin said. "When I told my mom and dad about it, they thought it was a great idea. They're not worried about the frozen pizzas at all."

"Really?" Joe asked.

Kevin pointed to a woman holding a pizza balloon.

"My mom says it's a great day for pizza," Kevin said. His eyes lit up. "Hey. I think I'll make that my headline."

"If you were mad at us," Joe said, "we don't blame you."

"I was," Kevin admitted. "That's why I didn't say 'hi' to you in the supermarket yesterday."

Frank grinned. "And we don't blame you for leaving that creepy message yesterday."

"What message?" Kevin asked.

"The pizza that said, 'Give Up Now!' " Joe said, surprised.

"Oh," Kevin said. "That was from Iola and her friends. I was at Pizza Paradise when they ordered it."

"I guess they were mad at us, too," Frank said. "For laughing at them."

Chet took his pizza recipe out of his pocket. "I guess I won't be needing this recipe anymore," he said sadly.

"Can I see it?" Kevin asked.

Chet handed Kevin the paper.

Kevin's mouth dropped open as he read the recipe. "Four kinds of cheese? Salami? Sweet peppers? Onions? Salsa?"

Kevin stared at Chet. "It has just the right amount of sweet and salty ingredients. I know a place that would love a pizza like this."

"Where?" Joe asked.

"Pizza Paradise," Kevin said.

Chet's eyes widened. "You mean it?"

"I'll show it to my mom," Kevin said.

"How do you like that?" Frank said as Kevin ran over to his mother. "We solved the case and got to enter the contest, too."

"And Chet here might be the next Chef Gorgonzola," Joe said.

"Is that neat or what?" Chet asked.

"Are you kidding?" Joe said. He put his arm around Chet's shoulder. "It's a dream come true!"